Tundra Books, an imprint of Penguin Random House Canada Young Readers,
a Penguin Random House Company

Library and Archives Canada Cataloguing in Publication

Winstanley, Nicola, author

  How to give your cat a bath / Nicola Winstanley ; illustrated by John Martz.

Issued in print and electronic formats.
ISBN 978-0-7352-6354-3 (hardcover).—ISBN 978-0-7352-6355-0 (ebook)

  I. Martz, John, 1978–, illustrator II. Title.

PS8645.I57278H69 2019   jC813'.6   C2018-900652-8
                                                 C2018-900653-6

Published simultaneously in the United States of America by Tundra Books of
Northern New York, an imprint of Penguin Random House Canada Young Readers,
a Penguin Random House Company

Library of Congress Control Number: 2018930309

Edited by Samantha Swenson
Designed by John Martz
The artwork in this book was drawn in ink and colored digitally.
The text was set in Century Std Book and Futura Std Extra Bold.

Printed and bound in China

www.penguinrandomhouse.ca

1 2 3 4 5   23 22 21 20 19

For my dear friend Anne,
who loves cats more than anyone I know
but never, ever tries to give her cats a bath
— NW

For Rachel, Honey and Mordecai
— JM

How to Give Your Cat a Bath

IN FIVE EASY STEPS

Nicola Winstanley tundra John Martz

How to Give Your Cat a Bath in Five Easy Steps

STEP ONE
Fill the bathtub with warm water.

That is too much water.

STEP ONE

Put a *little* warm water
in the bath.

Sigh.

STEP ONE

Put a little warm water
in the bath.

The water should come up
to your cat's knees.

STEP TWO

Put your cat in the —
wait, where is the cat?

Have you found
Mr. Flea yet?

Maybe we should start again.

STEP ONE
Find your —

Maybe we should start again.

STEP ONE
Find your —

Fine.

STEP ONE
Have some milk and cookies.

STEP TWO
Find your cat.

STEP THREE

Put your cat in the . . . hold on,
is the water still warm?

STEP FOUR
Hold your cat in one arm
and turn on the tap with your other —

STEP FIVE
Chase your cat
down the stairs!

STEP SEVEN
Turn off the water.

STEP EIGHT
Mop the floor.

STEP TEN
Find your cat.
Again.

How to Give Your Cat a Bath
in One Easy Step

STEP ONE
Sit quietly while your cat
licks himself clean.